WHEN THE RAINS COME

*For Annunciata, Beatrice, Charity and Dorothy
with huge admiration for the work they do and
for the love and joy they bring to it.*
TOM

*To Hélène, Marie and Ouiza for being amazing mums,
with love* MALIKA

First published in Great Britain in 2012 by Polygon, an imprint of Birlinn Ltd,
West Newington House, 10 Newington Road, Edinburgh EH9 1QS
www.polygonbooks.co.uk

ISBN: 978 1 84697 206 5
British Library Cataloguing-in-Publication Data
A catalogue record for this book is available on request from the British Library.

The publisher acknowledges investment from Creative Scotland
towards the publication of this volume.

Design by Teresa Monachino. Printed and bound in the EU.

WHEN THE RAINS COME

by

TOM POW

illustrated by

MALIKA FAVRE

Polygon

in association with MUMs

Beatrice walks along the dusty red road that leads into the village. She is holding the twins, Oscar and Jennifer, by their hands. The first person she sees is a man picking lemons from a tree. Each lemon is like a small, bright sun.

"*Moni. Muli bwanji?* Hello, how are you?" she says.

"*Ndili bwino. Muli bwanji?* I'm fine. How are you?"
he replies.

"Hot," says Beatrice. "It's a long and dusty road
to get here."

"Yes it is," says the Lemon Man.

"I'm looking for Grandmother Rose," says Beatrice.

"Well, you've almost found her. Past this tree,
on you go, and you're there," says the Lemon Man.

"*Zikomo.* Thank you," says Beatrice.

They find Grandmother Rose in her vegetable garden, chasing a hen from the fresh, green shoots. She flaps her arms like a large, colourful hen herself.

"Moni. Muli bwanji? Hello, how are you?" she says to Beatrice, puffing slightly and brushing the dust from her dress.

"Ndili bwino, zikomo. I'm fine, thank you," says Beatrice.

"I see you have the twins with you," says Grandmother Rose.

"Yes," says Beatrice. "They need someone to look after them now."

"I see," says Grandmother Rose. "Well, what can you do?" She bends down and strokes the shoulders of Oscar and Jennifer in turn. Jennifer's dress is too long for her. Her bare feet peep out from the hem of it like tiny fish.

"And there's a new baby too." Beatrice turns, so that Grandmother Rose can see the baby strapped to her back.

"But I have nothing to give a baby," says Grandmother Rose.

"Don't worry," says Beatrice, "I have milk for her here."

Grandmother Rose makes a coo-coo sound to the baby. "Does the baby have a name?" she asks.

"Yes," says Beatrice. "Her name is Grace."

In her hut, Grandmother Rose clears a space and lays Baby Grace down. Rays of sunlight come through the roof and the walls and dance on the earth floor. She goes to the new pump in the middle of the village and fills a green plastic basin with water, so that she can wash the dust from the three children – Oscar, Jennifer and Grace. She washes them till they shine.

"I'm going to look after you now," she tells them.

To settle the children on their first night, Grandmother Rose decides to tell them a story – one of her favourite stories about Tortoise.

Once, a long time ago, there was a great drought. There was no water anywhere. All the animals were weak with thirst and didn't know what to do. Tortoise, the least important of all the animals, suggested that they meet the next morning at the parched waterhole.

"Pah!" said Lion, "Since when did we pay any attention to what you say, Tortoise?"

But no one else knew what to do, and they were all so very thirsty. The next morning they were all at the waterhole – Lion, Elephant, Giraffe and every other animal you can think of.

"What we must do is stamp on the earth," said Tortoise. "If we stamp hard, the water will flow."

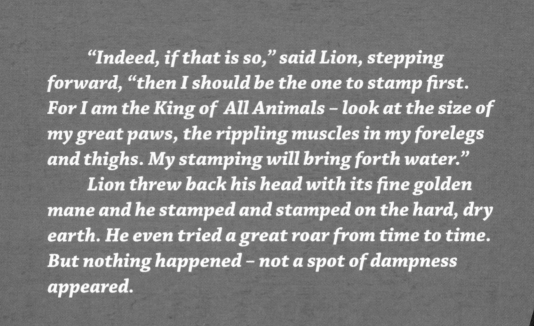

"Indeed, if that is so," said Lion, stepping forward, "then I should be the one to stamp first. For I am the King of All Animals – look at the size of my great paws, the rippling muscles in my forelegs and thighs. My stamping will bring forth water."

Lion threw back his head with its fine golden mane and he stamped and stamped on the hard, dry earth. He even tried a great roar from time to time. But nothing happened – not a spot of dampness appeared.

"Silly idea," said Lion. "Just as I told you it would be, coming from Tortoise."

But no one else knew what to do, so, next, Elephant stepped forward.

"Good try, Lion," he said. "Don't be too hard on yourself, for I think you'll find this is my kind of work. Who is heavier than me? Who can stamp with more force?"

And who is more tired than Oscar and Jennifer? Grandmother Rose asks herself. For they have both fallen into each other and are now fast asleep…

The next morning – and every morning – Oscar and Jennifer join the other children from the village. Each holds a bowl and a spoon for their porridge.

The porridge is cooked in the biggest pot you ever saw, stirred with a wooden paddle. The air is filled with the sweet smell of wood smoke.

The children line up for their porridge, the older children looking after the younger ones. Sometimes, they forget the queue and all the children squash together good-naturedly. But if anyone pushes Jennifer too hard, Oscar pushes him right back!

Grandmother Rose takes Grace with her, because Grace likes a spot of porridge, as well as her milk.

It's a very happy time and, after they have all eaten,
the helper mothers – Zuzika, Tadala and Bless –
sing and dance with the children:

Oh, we are happy today!

We are happy today!

It is special porridge with many good things in it
and, because of it, day by day, Oscar and Jennifer
and Baby Grace are growing stronger and stronger.

Oscar and Jennifer are becoming very good at keeping the hens and the goats off Grandmother Rose's new plants. Soon they are helping her to carry her potatoes, tomatoes and mangoes to market. It's not long before everyone who comes to market knows the children's names.

"*Moni. Muli bwanji, Oscar?* Hello, how are you? *Moni. Muli bwanji, Jennifer?* Hello, how are you?" they say.

"*Ndili bwino, zikomo.* I'm fine, thank you," Oscar and Jennifer answer together.

Grandmother Rose smiles brightly. And she smiles even more brightly, when people say, *"Moni. Muli bwanji, Grace?"* Baby Grace makes happy, gurgling sounds in reply.

One day, at the market, they hear a shout, *"Moni! Muli…"*

There is a bicycle – or is it a boat? – coming along the road. A blue sail billows around it. There is a laugh coming from the sail, then there is the sound of fear.

"Muli…Muli…oh…oh…oh!"

Beatrice – for it is she – passes the potato woman: "Oh…oh…oh!"

She passes the tomato woman: "Oh…oh…oh!"

Beatrice wibbles badly one way, wobbles another, hits a rut – and falls into a pile of watermelons.

She splits one, which grins back at her. But who is not grinning, once they realise she is not harmed?

Oscar and Jennifer help to pull her to her feet.
    "My new bicycle…" Beatrice says proudly.
    "…is beautiful," says Grandmother Rose.
    "Mmm," says Beatrice and she looks into the
clear eyes of the three children – Oscar, Jennifer
and Grace – and pinches the flesh of their arms.
    "And these children are beautiful too," she
says. "Growing healthier every day."

That night, Oscar and Jennifer are still laughing, when they remember Beatrice and her new bicycle falling into the watermelons. Grandmother Rose doesn't think they will sleep without a story. She will carry on with the story of Tortoise and the Drought and hope this time they can stay awake to hear the end of it.

"Remember," she begins, "how Lion stamped
and stamped, but could not bring water from
the dry earth. And how Elephant then stepped
forward…"

"Yes, yes, yes," say Oscar and Jennifer together.
"We remember! We remember!"

Elephant scraped the earth with his tusks and with his trunk, this way and that, till it was completely smooth.

He began to stamp and, when he stamped, the earth shook. The animals all looked from one to the other, as if to say, "Well, such stamping will surely bring forth water."

But all that Elephant managed was to stir up a huge amount of dust. Soon the animals were coughing and spluttering – but there was not a spot of dampness.

"You're right, Lion," said Elephant, "a silly idea. Why did we ever listen to Tortoise?"

But no one else knew what to do, so, next, Giraffe stepped forward. She was sure that, with her long powerful legs, she would bring forth water. But, for all her stamping – elegant though it was – there was not, in the end, a spot of dampness on the earth.

Giraffe turned away, muttering something about what a ridiculous idea it was to listen to Tortoise. But her head was so far above everyone else's, it was hard to make out the exact words.

All that stamping and not a spot of dampness. That was what all the animals were thinking. Or, maybe, there was a hair's breadth of dampness, a tiny line that only Tortoise - being the least and the lowest of all the animals - could see.

The dampness was rising from a spring of water deep within the earth. All the stamping and the thumping of Lion, Elephant and Giraffe had brought it very close to the surface.

Next to step forward was Tortoise himself.

"Tortoise himself," says Grandmother Rose.
But it is too late. The excitement of Beatrice and
her new bicycle has worn out Oscar and Jennifer
and they are fast asleep - fast asleep at the most
exciting part of the story!

The twins are getting stronger and they are learning too. Every morning, after porridge and after dancing, they sit on the floor of the shelter and Promise teaches the children the days of the week and the months of the year. You can hear them every morning:

Mon-day,
Tues-day,
Wednes-day,
Thurs-day...

Jan-uary,
Feb-ruary,
March,
Ap-ril...

Promise is one of the best dancers in the village – it is impossible for her not to move to the rhythm of the words. The children sit on their mats, chanting out the words, with a beat, as if they are the words of a song – all the small voices, sounding as one.

And so, the lives of Oscar and Jennifer and Baby Grace continue through the hot, dry months – growing, learning – until the rains begin. When the first rains come, freshening the earth, Grandmother Rose tells them she is now going to tell them the end of the story about Tortoise and the Drought.

"Remember," she says, "I told you how Lion had stamped and stamped and nothing had happened to the dry earth. Elephant had stamped and stamped; Giraffe had stamped and stamped. Yet still the earth was dry."

"Yes, yes, yes," say Oscar and Jennifer. "We remember! We remember!"

"Then you'll also remember that next to step forward was Tortoise himself. Well, whether you remember or nor, it was. Tortoise himself."

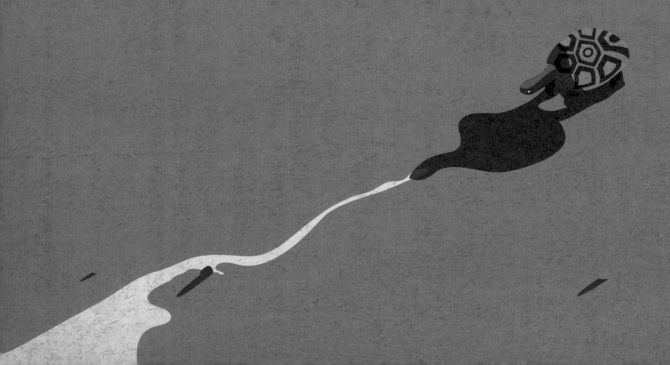

"You!" the animals laughed. "You, with your tiny feet. You will bring forth water, where the mighty lion, elephant and giraffe have all failed. Do you wonder that we laugh at you?"

"Yes, I know, like you all say, it's a silly idea," said Tortoise. "And you are all so much wiser than me. But as no one else has an idea what to do..."

Tortoise lifted his scaly little foot and he stamped on the earth. Not a sound was made, not a speck of dust raised. He stamped again with his left front foot and then again with his right.

From the dry earth, there came a tongue of water, licking its way through the dust. Each animal made its own sound of dismay and surprise: there were roars, trumpets, honks, squeals, barks and cheeps. It was hard to believe, but it was true. Tortoise, with his stamping, had brought forth water, when the other animals had failed.

The water was gushing up now, fountaining from the earth, till once again the waterhole was full and, thanks to Tortoise, all the animals could drink from it and bathe in it, from morning till night.

"What a clever idea!" said Lion, "As, of course, I always said it would be, coming from Tortoise".

"Pah!" said all the animals, "you were no wiser than any of us. But now we have learned that the least and the lowest among us can turn out to be the cleverest."

"And because of what he had done," says
Grandmother Rose, "Tortoise was made King."
"Did he make a good king?" Jennifer asks.
"Ah, well, that, my children, is another story."

The story of Tortoise and the Drought becomes
Oscar's and Jennifer's favourite story too. They
love when the animals can all have water to drink
at last, thanks to Tortoise.

But, at the moment, there is far too much
water in the village. As the rains fall, they find
every little crack in the roof of the hut. The
rains wash the earth away. Soon, little rivers run
everywhere.

Grandmother Rose does her best to keep her
hut clean, but it is very hard, for everywhere there
is red, sticky mud. Still, she washes the twins and,
while she washes Baby Grace, Jennifer holds an
umbrella up, for rain trickles through the roof.

"What can you do?" says Grandmother Rose,
shaking her head and smiling. "What can you do?"

She is washing the twins one day, when Beatrice arrives, pushing her bicycle through the mud, to see how the children are getting on.

"*Moni. Muli bwanji?* Hello, how are you?" says Beatrice.

"*Ndili bwino. Muli bwanji?* I'm fine. How are you?" says Grandmother Rose.

"I'm fine," says Beatrice. "But what's happening here?"

Grandmother Rose just holds her hands up to the sky and then points to the hens sheltering in a corner of the hut.

"What can you do?" she says.

"Tortoise would know what to do!" says Oscar.
"Well, I know someone else who will know
what to do," says Beatrice.

When Beatrice returns, the Lemon Man is with her.

"O.K.," says the Lemon Man, whose name is Sam, "Beatrice, when it stops raining, which it will do very soon, I need to borrow your bicycle. Oscar and Jennifer can help me."

Sam returns later with a stack of fresh, dry straw. He balances it on the seat and on the handlebars of the bicycle. Oscar and Jennifer hold the edges, so it does not fall off.

Sam takes off all the old straw and begins to thatch the hut again, taking care that the thatch is thick and tight.

"Now," says Grandmother Rose, when Sam has finished, "we're going to have a feast to celebrate our new roof. *Chambo* – fish, fresh from Lake Malawi."

"A sunshine feast!" says Sam.

"And after it, Grandmother Rose," says Oscar, "perhaps you could tell Beatrice and Sam the story of Tortoise and the Drought."

"If they'd like to hear it," says Grandmother Rose. "But I've told that story so often. I think you and Jennifer should tell it tonight."

"Can we?" says Oscar with excitement.

"Why ever not?" says Grandmother Rose. "Don't stories belong to everyone?"

"Would you like to hear us tell the story, Baby Grace?" says Jennifer

"Sure she would," says Sam.

And Baby Grace gurgles happily.

That night, it is the last of the rains. But, with its new roof, Grandmother Rose's hut is so dry that Oscar, Jennifer and Baby Grace dream that Tortoise and all his friends come to them there, seeking shelter.

"But how did you know about this hut?"
asks Lion.
"I dreamed it," says Tortoise.
And all the animals nod, knowing that King Tortoise is surely the wisest creature in the whole wide world.

A NOTE ABOUT MUMs AND ABOUT MALAWI

Malawi is often called the "sunshine heart of Africa".
Here, you can see it on the map. Scotland has very
close links with Malawi. Like Scotland, it is a very
beautiful country.

MUMs (Malawi's Underprivileged Mothers)
helps mums and their children in Malawi to have
a better start in life. It has helped mothers in
Lilongwe, the capital of Malawi, to have their babies
more safely. Because of MUMs, in five villages
in and around Lilongwe, children are fed phala
– nutritious porridge – for breakfast five days a
week. It's hard to learn if you're hungry! Sometimes
children, like Oscar and Jennifer in the story, have
no one to look after them properly. They become so
hungry, they may be taken into care until they are
strong enough to return to the village. Once back in
the village, it's important that they are well fed and
that they have the chance to go to school. I hope
you have enjoyed this story and that it's told you
something about the work of MUMs.

If you would like to find out more about MUMs
projects, go to www.mumsrecipes.org

Thank you for buying this book. By doing so,
you are supporting mums and children in Malawi.

Linda McDonald
(Founder of the MUMs charity)

MUMs Scottish Registered Charity Number is SC037759